THOMAS & FRIENDS™

Thomas and the Piglets

Thomas loved all the farms on Sodor, but his favourite of all was Farmer Trotter's pig farm!

Thomas loved seeing the pigs playing in the mud and hearing them **oink** happily as he passed by.

One day, Farmer Trotter had some exciting news.

"One of my pigs is going to have piglets today," he told Thomas. "Could you fetch some soft straw for them from Farmer McColl's farm?"

"Of course," Thomas replied.

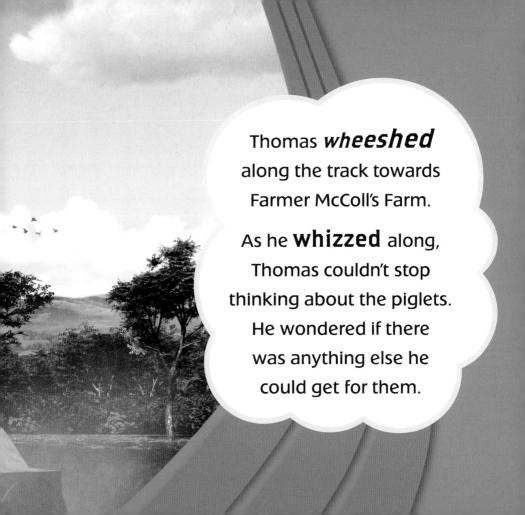

Thomas *wheeshed* along the track towards Farmer McColl's Farm.

As he **whizzed** along, Thomas couldn't stop thinking about the piglets. He wondered if there was anything else he could get for them.

As Thomas **puffed** past the Dairy, he saw Percy collecting the milk.

"May I have some milk for Farmer Trotter's piglets?" Thomas asked.

"Of course," Percy replied, and some milk was loaded into Thomas' truck.

Thomas thanked Percy and he **chuffed** away.

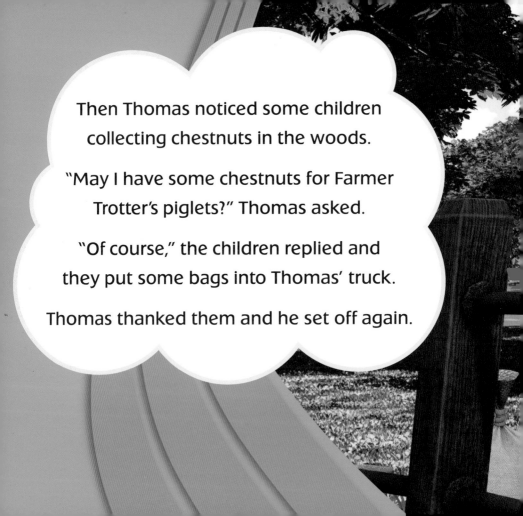

Then Thomas noticed some children collecting chestnuts in the woods.

"May I have some chestnuts for Farmer Trotter's piglets?" Thomas asked.

"Of course," the children replied and they put some bags into Thomas' truck.

Thomas thanked them and he set off again.

Finally, Thomas rolled into Farmer McColl's yard.

"You're late," the Farmer said crossly. "And your truck is full, so there's no room for the piglets' straw!"

Thomas hadn't thought about that.

"I'll quicky take these things to Farmer Trotter, then I'll come straight back for the straw," Thomas told him.

But when Thomas arrived at the pig farm, Farmer Trotter wasn't happy either.

"Piglets must have soft straw," he said. "And they'll be born **very soon!**"

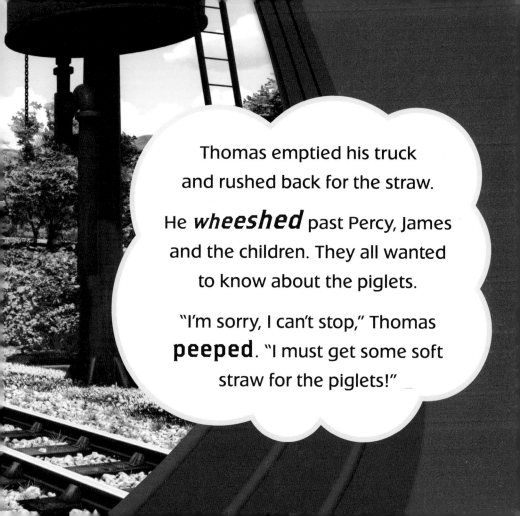

Thomas emptied his truck and rushed back for the straw.

He **wheeshed** past Percy, James and the children. They all wanted to know about the piglets.

"I'm sorry, I can't stop," Thomas **peeped**. "I must get some soft straw for the piglets!"

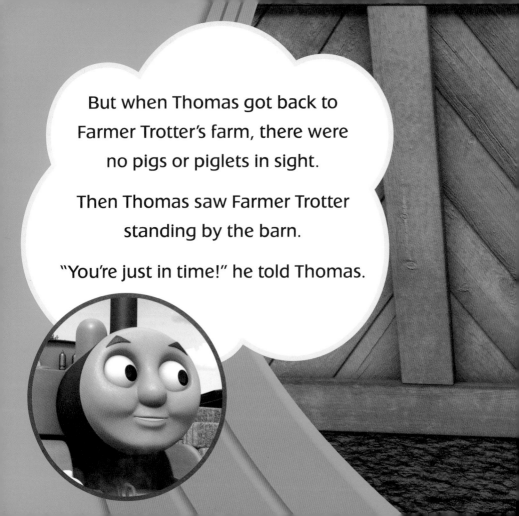

But when Thomas got back to Farmer Trotter's farm, there were no pigs or piglets in sight.

Then Thomas saw Farmer Trotter standing by the barn.

"You're just in time!" he told Thomas.

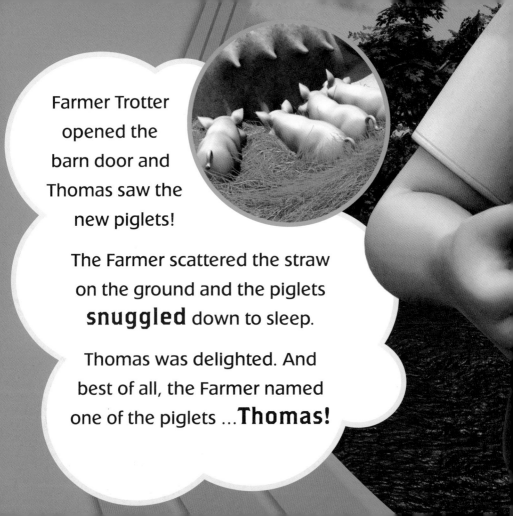

Farmer Trotter opened the barn door and Thomas saw the new piglets!

The Farmer scattered the straw on the ground and the piglets **snuggled** down to sleep.

Thomas was delighted. And best of all, the Farmer named one of the piglets ...**Thomas!**

PEEP! PEEP!

The End